T0146516

ALAINA

THE ANGEL SAVES THE DAY

KATISKA STEPHENS

authorHOUSE®

AuthorHouse™
1663 Liberty Drive
Bloomington, IN 47403
www.authorhouse.com
Phone: 1 (800) 839-8640

Published by AuthorHouse 06/17/2016

ISBN: 978-1-5246-1129-3 (sc)
ISBN: 978-1-5246-1128-6 (e)

Library of Congress Control Number: 2016908633

Print information available on the last page.

Little Alaina was very happy to finally receive her wings. She was granted them, because she did great things. She went before her master with tears in her eyes.

Little Alaina was very happy to be . . .
to new homes. She was again . . . then . . .
Now that she had new things. She went b . . .
her mama and went to her room.

Many could not understand why she cried. Alaina shared tears of joy, because her heart was full. She finally received an opportunity to help other little kids with problems on this earth endure.

With her mother and father by her side, she walked up to her master. He took her by the hand and led the way. He asked that all the other angels would join hands and pray.

After they prayed, Alaina was given a long sheet of paper that was written by hand. She looked at it as if she didn't understand. She was never told that she was getting any paper. She was just looking forward to receiving her wings. As she started reading the paper slowly, she looked up at her master and asked, "Why me?"

He told her that she was the chosen one that will receive her wings after her work is done. He told her that if she could successfully complete her mission on earth, she will be a very, very happy little angel. After her work is done, she was ordered to return to her master and receive her wings. She always did the right things, so she looked up at her master and asked, "how many and how long?'

He told her that it was two and it will take as long as it will take for them to find a place where they belong. Her parents and the other angels didn't know what they were talking about. They did know however that everything will be worked out. They knew that she was eventually going to receive her wings one day. Why?

Because they believed everything they prayed. They prayed with her for that to come to pass, and they knew that things that they prayed for sometimes don't happen as fast. Alaina left her master and began talking to the other angels that gathered around her. She told them that she had to be placed back on earth.

She had to help out God's children so they could find peace. She had to help them with their every need. Alaina was assigned to Alabama Street. She had to set the little children free.

She had two children that she had to save.
She was given the paper to carry with her so
she could be familiar with what they requested
when they prayed.

Ashley, a little girl on the street has
everything that she needs.

She is 9 years old and always wears designer clothes. She goes to private schools and was bought everything she ever wanted. Each and every day she wore something new. In an instance, Ashley's whole life changed. She started having headaches that were unbearable.

She couldn't understand where they were coming from. Her parents took her to many doctors, but the headaches didn't stop. They became worse. Her parents and the ones that love her were sharing great remorse.

They finally took her to a specialist. He ran many tests. Weeks passed and the test results came back. The test showed that she had Leukemia, and something needs to be done about it right away.

Her parents looked at each other and they both began to cry. All they were thinking about was how their life would change once their only child died. Ashley's parents had all the money in the world, but they could not buy better health for their beautiful little girl. Ashley didn't understand what leukemia was but she wanted to know.

She began asking her mom questions about it, but her mom couldn't answer them without crying. She always walked away, went into another room, and closed the door. She didn't want Ashley to see her cry. Ashley had a prayerful grandmother.

She always took Ashley to church. Ashley remembered the words that her grandmother gave her while she was on this earth. Ashley's grandmother died last year. Ashley missed her so much, but she knew that her grandmother was in a better place.

That's where Ashley's grandmother always told her that she would be. She taught Ashley how to pray. She read the Bible with Ashley each and every day.

Since Ashley wasn't getting any answers at home, she decided to seek a Higher Power and believed that He would come. She knew that if she prayed, she would be alright. Ashley began to go into her closet every day after school and pray until she cried.

She asked God to heal her and take her sickness away. She asked Him to please hear her while she prayed. Ashley kept praying, but her little body started to get weak. Her headaches were still there and she found it hard to speak.

Little Ashley started focusing more on her sickness and took her eyes off what she was praying for. She started losing hope. She no longer believed that the Higher Power was going to come in and heal her. She no longer could go to school, and she had to be admitted to the hospital with other little kids.

Ashley became a bitter little girl. She told the little girl that she was in the room with that she always prayed and look what God did. The little girl told her that God does not destroy his own.

She told her that He will heal her as long as she let go. Ashley didn't understand what she had to let go, so she asked the little girl, "What do I need to let go?" The little girl told Ashley that she needs to let go all her anger and disbelief. She told Ashley to let go the words of this world, because only God knows what's going to happen to her.

She also told Ashley that she needs to think about what her grandmother told her and remember all the things that His son died for. Ashley began to cry, but suddenly stopped and asked the little girl how she knew what her grandmother told her. The little girl just looked at Ashley and smiled. She didn't answer Ashley's question, but she did tell her that she just needs to know that she is a very blessed child.

The nurse walked into the room to check on Ashley. She gave Ashley another IV and told her to think positive. She told Ashley that she is surrounded by people who show her a lot of love. Ashley smiled and told the nurse that she would do her best.

The nurse started to walk out the room, turned around and told Ashley to get some rest. The little girl in Ashley's room slowly got up and out of bed. She walked over to Ashley. She picked up the brush off the table next to Ashley's hospital bed and began brushing Ashley's beautiful long hair out of her face.

The little girl grabbed Ashley's hand and said, "Ashley, pray with me".

The little girl told Ashley that before they prayed, she had to believe, have faith and know that she will be set free. Ashley looked into the little girl eyes and said, "I Believe". The little girl began to pray...

"Dear Lord, I come to you just as I

am and as humble as I know how,

I ask that you will heal my

new friend right now,

I ask that you will give her

strength to endure,

Lord, give her a cure,

Touch her Lord in every way,

Heal her completely on this day,

Renew her mind and give her peace,

I profess that she will have

victory over this disease,

In Jesus name, Amen

For You Only I stand"

Ashley couldn't understand what came over her at that very instance. Ashley began to cry. It was a great feeling! It was a feeling that Ashley never felt before. Ashley stretched her hands toward the ceiling and began to ask for more.

She wanted more of that warm, comforting feeling that she felt inside. In her mind, she was taken to a new place. A place where there's rest and serenity. Ashley began praising God.

Tears kept flowing down her pretty little face. Ashley believed that she had work to do and will be here on this earth for many more years. When Ashley stopped shouting, she looked over to the little girl's bed. The bed was made up like the little girl was never in it.

She looked around and tried to figure out where the little girl had gone. She was feeling stronger and had an appetite. Her headache was gone and she began to speak right; but Ashley didn't know where the little girl that helped her had gone. Ashley finally fell asleep. She felt so much peace and didn't feel alone.

Ashley woke up early the next morning to her mother's voice. She was talking to the doctor who wanted her to make a choice. Ashley didn't know what choice her mother had to make, but she knew that she was already healed and didn't want her mom to make any mistakes. Ashley asked her mom what the doctor want her to do.

Her mom looked at her and said, "He wants me to decide how we will take care of you" "Will we leave you in the hospital or will we allow you to come home with us sick and bring you in for chemotherapy." Ashley didn't know what chemotherapy was but she knew that she was already healed. Ashley told her mom that she felt better and to ask the doctor to run more tests.

Her mom told her that she would. Ashley's mom left the room to get the doctor. A nurse came in Ashley's room and said, "Ashley I am here to take you." Ashley replied, "Take me where?"

The nurse said, "Downstairs to run more tests; your new gown and slippers are over there." Ashley got out of bed like she was in no pain. The nurse was totally amazed. She saw how sick Ashley had been, but suddenly she looked better and had strength.

Ashley told the nurse that she didn't need any help getting dressed at all. She said, "Don't worry, I won't fall." The nurse stepped back and allowed Ashley to dress herself. After Ashley dressed, they both went downstairs.

The tests were done, and the doctor put a rush order in for the results so he would know what else he needed to do. Ashley stayed three more days in the hospital, as well as could be. She still wondered where her new friend had gone. She missed her even though she didn't know her that well. Ashley knew that they shared a bond and an inspirational story to tell.

Ashley's mom arrived at the hospital as usual, bright and early with a smile on her face. She told Ashley that she couldn't wait until she got to leave that place. Ashley looked into her mothers eyes and said, "Mom it will be soon" "God will see me through". After Ashley said that, the door opened, and the doctor entered the room.

He had a puzzled look on his face and said, "I need to talk to the both of you." Her mom suddenly started crying out loud and said, "Lord, what should I do?" Ashley was surprised to hear her mom talk to God. Her mom never went to church and her grandmother always prayed them through. The doctor said, "Wait, it's not bad news; I have the test results and I want to share them with you."

Ashley grabbed her mother's hand and they waited patiently to hear what the doctor had to say. He said, "There is no trace of leukemia in Ashley" "I don't understand but the results are here in my hand written plain as day." Ashley's mother started to cry again, except this time, she cried tears of joy.

Ashley already knew what the results were going to be and what they wouldn't find. The doctor told Ashley that she was free to go home. The two of them left, and Ashley looked in the sky and said, "Thank you Lord for a job well done."

Darius is a 13 year old boy that also lives on Alabama Street. He is being raised by a single mother of three. She works a full time job and goes to school. She always pray and go to church so that God would guide her through.

Darius always saw his mom praying and praising God. He knew that she always put God in charge. One day Darius got home from school and saw his mom's car outside. He wondered why she was home and not at work at that time.

Darius' grandmother kept him and his two sisters while their mom was away. Their grandmother wasn't needed to be there on that day. Darius walked into the house and noticed that the door to his mom's room was shut tightly. Darius knocked on the door and called his mother. He said, "Mom, this is Darius, I'm here."

His mom waited a few minutes and then she opened the door. Darius looked at her and gave her a big hug. He asked, "Mom, what are you here for?" She said, "Baby I lost my job today and I have no one to help me."

Darius was too young to understand how much pain his mom was in. He did know that his mom always worked to support their family financially. Their dad never gave them anything. He hasn't been around now for quite some time.

Months had passed and his mom became more and more sad. Their meals became smaller and their clothes no longer would fit. They were given used clothes from other families but were teased by the other kids.

When Darius and his sisters wore the used clothes to school, the children whose clothes they were given would say, "Hey you're wearing my old clothes, my mom gave them to you."

"You are poor and don't have anything to eat."

"You don't even have good shoes on your feet."

Darius and his sisters walked away with their heads down. They often cried when no one else was around. Darius couldn't remember the last time he saw his mother pray. She didn't praise God like she did before.

It was strange because she used to do it every day. Darius asked his mom why she didn't pray anymore. She looked at him with tears in her eyes and walked into her room and shut the door.

Darius knew that someone needed to pray in their house, so that everything would eventually work out. He started praying every day after school.

He believed that God would see them through. Darius felt alone because he no longer had friends. The friends he thought he had, began teasing him with the other kids.

On the playground he played all alone and wondered why the other kids weren't treating him right. One day during recess, Darius saw a new student that needed a friend.

She had long hair and beautiful skin. Darius walked over and introduced himself to her. The girl smiled and told him that she wanted to know more. She wanted to know his likes and dislikes. She wanted to know his dreams and whether or not he fights.

She wanted to know if he did well in school. She wanted to know everything! Darius was confused and wondered why she asked so many questions as if she cares. He wondered why she just met him but already has told him that she will always be there for him.

Darius went home that afternoon and prayed again. His mother's attitude was getting worse by the day. He became close to the little girl. She was his only friend, and he trusted her.

He told her about his mother losing her job and feeling sad all the time. He told her about how he prays everyday for the Lord to change her mind. Darius found out that the little girl also prayed. He found out that she went to church every Sunday with her family and believed God!

Her family puts God first in everything that they do. Days later the little girl walked up to Darius and asked him to join her in prayer. She grabbed his hand and told him to believe whatever she said. The little girl began to pray....

"Lord, we come to you on this day,

Trusting and believing that

you will make a way,

You know Darius' mom situation and we

know that there's nothing too hard for you,

We trust and believe that you

will see her through,

Help Darius stay strong and

encouraged everyday,

In Jesus name, I pray…"

Darius' eyes filled with tears, but he knew deep inside that he didn't need to fear. He knew that his mother and his sisters were going to be just fine. He knew that his mom would indeed have a new mind. The teachers signaled for the children to come inside.

Darius looked for his little friend so she could walk with him to the classroom. She disappeared in an instance and he didn't know where she had gone. He was just praying with her and only looked away for a second. "Where is she?" he kept thinking to himself.

Darius finally began to walk inside. He stopped and took one last look around to see if he would see his friend. He realized that she was really gone. He entered the classroom and walked to the teacher's desk.

He said, "Mrs. Jones, there's something that I must ask." "Where did the little girl go that was in our class with the long hair?" He added, "You know. She is new and used to sit right there."

Darius started pointing at the seat next to him. The teacher looked puzzled and asked, "Darius, do you have an imaginary friend?" Darius responded, "No she was real; we played together and she wiped away all my tears." "Tears?" The teacher replied.

"Yes, I trusted her and I told her a lot of things." Darius said.

The teacher told Darius that they haven't had a new student in their class. She then asked Darius if he needed to talk to the counselor because it was time to begin math.

Darius told her that he didn't need to talk to anyone and that he was okay. Darius was still confused about what happened to his little friend. He waited anxiously for the school day to end. Darius arrived at home as usual.

When he walked to the door, he heard his mother's voice praying and praising God just like she did before. He smiled and enjoyed what he was hearing at the time. His sisters walked behind him as he entered the house. Their faces also began to shine. Their mother greeted them with a hug and a kiss on the cheek.

She said, "Babies please forgive me. I know that I haven't really been there for you during the time that I was going through. You are my rock and the reason why I do what I do. I only want the best for you."

At the same time, the three children said, "Mom, we forgive you." Darius added, "Mom God will see us through. I prayed when you no longer prayed. I believed when you no longer believed.

I praised when you no longer praised."
Darius' mom grabbed his hand and led him
to the sofa. She sat down, and he sat down
beside her. She began telling him how proud
she was of him.

He began to tell his mother about his new friend. His words were cut off by the sound of the telephone. His mother answered the phone and was talking softly but when she hung up the phone, she began singing. "Victory is mine, victory is mine, victory today is mine!

Darius smiled, because he knew that God had given his mom her new mind. She came in the room to join her children. She said, "Kids, that was human resources, I am going back to work!"

"They offered me a new job getting paid more than ever and I start next week; we won't have to depend on anyone but God." "He will never leave us."

Everything was back to normal with Darius and his family. They were happy and living in perfect peace.

Alaina's work on this earth was now done. She told her parents that she actually had fun. She completed her missions and was ready to receive her wings. She longed for this day to come before her King.

With praises coming out her mouth and while others began to shout, she walked before the King once again. He said, "Alaina, job well done." "Here are your wings." "Fly free and at all times and in all things remember to acknowledge me."

About the Author

I am Katiska Stephens. I am an inspirational poetry writer. I also write children's books. I live in Columbus, Georgia, with my husband, Hosie, who is currently active in the military. I have two children, Darius and Traneisha. I also have a granddaughter, Treasure. God gave me a gift to inspire all people. My writings are to inspire and motivate people. I love to spend time with family and make a difference in people's lives. God is good, and I know Him for myself. I pray that through my work, others will begin to know Him for themselves.

Printed in the United States
By Bookmasters

Printed in the United States
By Bookmasters